THERE'S A DINOSAUR UNDER MY BED

Written by Judith Olson

Illustrated by Marilyn Jacobson

Written by Judith Olson

Illustrated by Marilyn Jacobson

Published by
Red Squirrel Publishing L.L.C.
Ramsey, Minnesota

HARDCOVER - ISBN: 978-1-7366392-1-4

Library of Congress Control Number: 2021906760

Light of the Moon, Inc.
Partnering with self-published authors since 2009
Book Design/Production/Consulting
Carbondale, Colorado • www.lightofthemooninc.com

For my grandson,
Steven "Kody," AKA T-Rex.

May you always find a dinosaur under your bed.

"Be strong and courageous.
Do not be afraid; do not be discouraged,
for the Lord your God will be with you
wherever you go."
~ Joshua 1:9

"It's all in your head," is what my mom said.

But I know I have a dinosaur under my bed.

When my room is dark and I can't see,

He climbs on my bed and sleeps next to me.

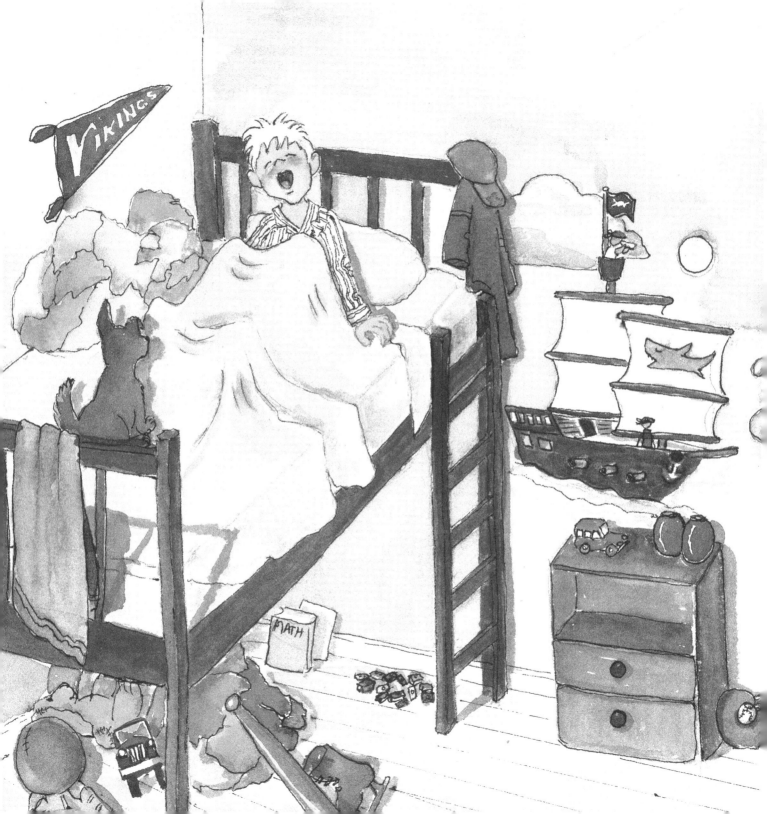

If I cover my head trying to hide,

There he is right at my side.

When the lights are off and I am under my sheet,

I can feel his tail touching my feet.

My pillow is soft until he arrives.

Then it's all lumpy and bumpy inside.

Before too long I get pushed on the floor.

My room is so dark I can't find the door.

His feet are so big I stumble and trip,

Banging my head and cutting my lip.

I yell, "MOM, COME HERE!"

She says, "Kody, you heard what I've said!"

"But Mom, there's a dinosaur under my bed."

"You know that's not true, I told you before.

Now crawl into bed, leave a crack in the door."

"Mom, PLEASE come to see that it's true.

See, he's right there next to my shoe."

Mom comes into my room and begins to chuckle.

On my lumpy, bumpy pillow is my new cowboy buckle.

Mom checks the floor where I tripped on his toes.

Nothing is there but my shoes and my clothes.

The tail at my feet that feels like a log,

Is Lole my shepherd, my new puppy dog.

My pants, shirt, and socks are rolled in a ball,

Planted firmly between my blanket and the wall.

"I am sure he's here somewhere, look, you'll see,

That scaly ole dinosaur that keeps bothering me."

Hiding behind my mom, I bend down to look.

To find that dinosaur, and not one in a book!

We find my stuffed dog (Giraffe) and an old pet rock,

As well as a math assignment I guess I forgot.

My hammer, my knife, my new mittens from Gram.

Even the bat I used to hit that grand slam.

There are Legos and cars—so much stuff on the floor,

No wonder I had trouble finding the door.

But the dinosaur is missing, nowhere to be found,

I was sure we would find him but he made not a sound.

It's clear he has been here keeping my things,

Look, he's even taken my mood rings.

Mom smiled a smile only my mom can do.

"Kody, it seems this stuff all belongs to you!

Morning is coming and you know the rule.

Clean your room when you get home from school."

Mom cleared off my bed and straightened my pillow.

"Now under these sheets, my sleepy blonde fellow."

I give Mom a kiss and settle in for the night.

Lole, Giraffe, and I are cuddled up tight.

I know Mom said it was all in my head,

But I will dream of the dinosaur under my bed.

ABOUT THE AUTHOR

Judith Olson enjoys using a child's imagination,
and her own, to tell stories to her grandchildren.
This is the second book she has written for them.
The first is *I Love You More Than Pigs Love Mud*.
Her goal is to write a story for each of her grandchildren
based on the stories she has told them over the years.

ABOUT THE ILLUSTRATOR

Marilyn Jacobson is an award-winning artist
and paints in a variety of styles, from realistic to whimsical.
She has illustrated numerous children's books
in which the characters expressed emotions and personality.
See more of Marilyn's fun and colorful art at
1-marilyn-jacobson.pixels.com

CPSIA information can be obtained
at www.ICGtesting.com
Printed in the USA
BVHW022032170521
607268BV00015B/1669